Louisa
The
Poisoner

LOUISA
The
POISONER

by Tanith Lee

illustrated by
George Barr

The Wildside Press
Berkeley Heights, NJ

LOUISA THE POISONER

For more information, contact:

The Wildside Press
522 Park Avenue
Berkeley Heights, NJ 07922

ISBN: 1-880448-50-5

March Mire lay at the heart of the great moors, a swamp so dangerous that none but fools would venture into it, and seldom did they come out. There were however local legends of persons who lived within the mire itself, creatures that knew the two or three safe paths across the mud. Generally they were said to be mad people, for if not crazy to begin with, the gloom, vapours, and weird sights of the bog soon sent them that way. They dwelled in lopsided hovels perched upon the quag and made their soup from peculiar plants, ate frogs even, and perhaps godlessly worshipped the stars. Now and then tales were told of encounters on the moor with phantom phosphorescent dogs and men who had webbed hands and feet, and mostly all the stories were as apocryphal as these.

Nevertheless, it was true, Louisa lived with her aunt in a cottage on the mire and for nineteen years knew no other life.

Her mother had died giving her birth, and her father perished some time before. The aunt took over the cottage and the baby and ruled both in her own individual style. It had happened that a traveller once penetrated the mire and came on the cottage—although whether he ever escaped from either is not known. He had a bag of books concerning etiquette and the proper manners of gentlefolk, and this, after he had mysteriously vanished from her life, the aunt read voraciously over and over and so learned of in minute detail. These lessons were then passed on to the child Louisa. From the age of three or four she was trained in how to sit, stand, walk and talk, how to clothe herself, blow her nose, and eat her food, all with imaginary implements—the cutlery and linen of the cottage were sparse—how even to comb and dress her long black hair, and when and where to lift her hazel eyes. And if the child failed at her studies, the aunt would beat her, using in the early days a softish switch of grass, but graduating to a set of sticks at the sight of which a strong man might have quailed. Let it be said that after the age of nine, Louisa was never beaten again, for she had become quite perfect.

Aside from her obsession with comportment, the aunt was a slattern. The cottage was thick with filth, the few garments and utensils ragged and rusty. Only the hale constitutions of both the woman and the girl kept them alive and well in the midst of this sea of germs.

On the other hand illness might not have mattered, for the aunt was a herbalist of uncanny ability. Day long and night long she roved about the bog gathering flowers and weeds, ferns and roots, and slimy excrescences without name or number. Unlike the skills of etiquette, her knowledge here was not passed on to Louisa. On returning from a foray the aunt would put herself into a mildewed chair and give instructions. "Make me a cup of parsley tea. Let me see you walk. Now turn and look at that wall. Now step over that crack. Yes, yes. That's right."

The evening arrived however that was Louisa's nineteenth birthday—for she had come into the world at one quarter to nine of a summer's dusk.

The aunt had been out as usual, gleaning from the mire, and as usual Louisa had got on with her few allotted chores and otherwise spent the time looking in the mirror over the mantle. For this was Louisa's hobby. In her strange and boring life, she had found one interest, her beautiful face, her long black satin hair, the elegant patterns she made as she moved in the stances her aunt had grafted to her. When the aunt set her tasks, Louisa would get enjoyment in watching her own graceful hands at the work. It was true they were brown from the sun, but even so a better pair of hands could not be imagined. "Put on your rings," the aunt would say, and Louisa would put on the twists of bark and paper, and herself imagine the great fiery rubies and weeping sapphires pictured in the books.

So, Louisa was looking at herself in the mirror when her aunt returned from the mire, out of breath and croaking like a frog.

"Louisa—Louisa—"

"Yes, Aunt."

"At last, I found them. I found them in the reeds. For twenty years I've searched them out, I knew they must be there. And now, now I have them, plucked in my basket. The key to enormous dreams."

Louisa said again, in her phonetically taught, accentless and cultured tones, "Yes, Aunt." and went back to the mirror. Unlike her aunt she was not a slut. Her person and the mirror (as it were, her territory) were always as clean and pristine as she could make them.

The aunt began to brew a foul smelling concoction on the range, and presently Louisa left the cottage. She stood and admired the stars, and the will-o'-the-wisps flitting on the bog, though they were a poor substitute.

It was with slight amazement that Louisa discovered her aunt calling her back, near midnight, into the house. Never before had this tyrant shown any need to share her work with the simples. Now she seemed overbrimming, like her cauldron. At least the awful smell had gone. Indeed, a faint fragrance, indefinable, hung over the cottage's congealed air.

"Louisa, sit down."

"Yes, Aunt."

"Do you see?" The aunt held up a rare glass phial, scoured abnormally of muck. In it was a colourless oily liquid.

"Oh yes, Aunt."

"There are three things that grow in March Mire," said the aunt, in a silly sing-song voice, her eyes half closed, "and that grow nowhere else together, and seldom anywhere. Find them in one spot, take them and make them up. From them comes this dew. Oh Louisa. Listen carefully. This stuff grants the gift of death."

Louisa widened her eyes but she was not actually impressed. Death was everywhere in the mire and especially often in her aunt's nasty bottles.

"Listen," said the aunt again, "the poison in this bottle leaves no trace as it kills. In the world beyond the mire this can mean much. I've told you, there are towns along the moors, and great houses piled up with money and jewels. If every cobweb on that ceiling was changed to bank notes it would be nothing to them."

"And the streets and roofs are paved with gold," said Louisa.

"Yes," said the aunt, who had never been there, or had forgotten. "What we'll do is this. Tomorrow we'll leave the mire by Ghost Horse Path. We'll seek for just such a rich place. Then I'll know how to go on. You shall pretend to be a lost lady, as I've trained you. I'll act your slave—or servant, if they don't have slaves any more. But you'll do as I say, and our fortune will be made for ever."

"But how, Aunt?"

"They'll fall in love and make over their goods through wills, which I've told you of. And then I'll see them off."

"But Aunt," said Louisa, shyly, "do you need me? It's you who have the poison."

"Need you? Yes. You're the morsel that baits my trap. It's you will catch the eye, and you that will convince them you're a darling angel fallen from heaven."

"Tomorrow?" asked Louisa.

"Yes, and early," said the aunt. Her head nodded. She had had a busy day. She murmured drowsily, "I'll tell you how it is. One drop from the phial, only one. Tasteless and scentless and makes indeed the dish more delicious and the cup nicer. One drop and they die a painless easy death. But two drops and they die in agony—that's for enemies."

"And three drops?" asked Louisa.

"Three drops," said the aunt, her eyes shut, "and there's fire."

11

"Fire?"

But the aunt only mumbled, "Make me some fennel tea before I sleep."

So Louisa put on the kettle, and the aunt being already asleep, Louisa slipped out of her fingers the phial and let fall two crystal drops from it into the cracked tea cup.

"Here's you tea, aunt."

"Why, how good this tastes. I never tasted anything so good. The taste of victories to come."

Louisa asked her aunt if she might take the phial and place it on the table. The aunt agreed and got up to go to bed. Half way there she gave a loud cough and then bent right over backwards in a hoop. She screamed and her spine snapped and serpents of blood leapt from her lips.

Louisa watched with great interest. What her aunt had told her was quite true.

She waited until the spasms, asphyxia and bleeding ceased, and then she went to bed. Louisa found her couch far more comfortable without the aunt snoring beside her. The aunt was completely silent now.

In the morning early, Louisa got up, washed herself and tidied her rags, combed out her hair and ate a piece of grass seed bread. Then she put the phial of poison in her pocket and went out along Ghost Horse Path, which her aunt had shown her long ago in order to frighten her. By night a headless luminous horse was sometimes seen there, jumping the quag and flying through the air, but by day only bog myrtle, butterflies and kestrels appeared.

The Path ended at the edge of March Mire, and Louisa emerged from it and stepped forth on the great moors.

These piled in all directions, greyish and purplish green, and tawny with bracken, with ancient rocks in the distance and a low sky of moving rock-like cloud. A storm approached and Louisa had never been so far into the world. She walked boldly out into it and after the blowing clouds. And presently she reached a broad and sprawling road. To her surprise it was not paved with gold. This gave her some idea of caution. The lessons of her aunt were immaculate only to a point. She would need a little extra care.

ightning flashed and thunder crashed above as Louisa sat at the roadside on a red stone. She had seen, below in a valley of the winding road, a dark carriage hurtling through the driving rain, and she knew that destiny gave the carriage to her and gave her to the carriage. In her mirror-like mind was an image of her own self as she would be seen, slender and peerless in a cloak of raven hair, under the scourge of heaven. The red stone was useful too, as it stood out very clearly even in bad weather.

The carriage raged up on to the hill behind six galloping jet black horses. It bore down on her like a thunderbolt. Louisa lifted her arms in a vague appealing gesture. The carriage came level, drenched her, scorched her with its wind, and dashed past. Louisa sat down. Half a mile away, with much rearing of the horses and shouts, the carriage drew up, lurched, and was brought around. The horses bounded back to the stone. The carriage was level again. The door, whose window was curtained in salmon velvet, and on which there was a crest in gold, was opened. Two men stared out at Louisa in the rain.

"By God," said the young fat one, "a mermaid."

The old thin one shook his long grey locks. "A beggar. Poor wretch."

Louisa rose again and went to the carriage door like a black swan over a river. She put out her marvelous hand and raised her flower face. "Sir, I'm a lady," said Louisa, "who is lost on the moor. I have no one in the world."

*   *   *

13

Maskullance Manor had long dominated the moor. Its foundations had been laid two centuries previously, and since then the house had grown up and over itself like a prodigious stone vegetable. It had towers at two corners and vast stacks of mullioned glass casements, and everywhere upon the masonry were the architectural puns of eight generations of Maskullances, concerning masks, skulls, and lances. Louisa liked it very well, even though the roof was not paved with anything more than slates. One golden weathervane consoled her, and a devilish golden ram's mask above the main door.

The approach to the manor was also quite impressive. First the carriage leapt through a village of tiny houses and squirreline shops, where, even in the downpour, villagers emerged from the inn to doff their caps. Half a mile on, a park had been coaxed from the moors, and nourished oaks and beech copses, a lake, and, against the house, sombre gardens of topiary filled with herds of screaming turquoise peacocks.

On the journey Louisa was asked questions.

It was the old man who asked most of them, and Louisa knew by her fox-like instinct that he did not really care what she replied. For the old man had fallen at once deeply in love with her. Nor did Louisa differentiate between types of love. She only saw that he looked at her just as she had always looked at herself in the mirror.

The young man, however, who asked far less, was far more concerned with answers and not at all with love.

"But where do you come from?" he had demanded, not calling her, either, by her name, as the old one had at once, on learning it.

"I can't say," said Louisa. She added, diligently, "Sir. My lips must remain sealed. Mine isn't a happy history. You would be sorry to hear it." Her aunt would have been proud of her, had she not been rotting quietly on the cottage floor.

14

"No, Bleston," said the old man, who had lace at his cuffs, a huge ruby carbuncle on his finger, a pearl pin for his stock. "When you find a fairy in the wood, you mustn't pry into her secrets."

"Fairy!" snorted Bleston, who was not only fat but ugly, with flushed face, thick pink lips, and repressed eyes. "I'll give her she speaks like a lady. But these clothes, the state of her!"

"Hush, Bleston. You are not polite."

The old man had asked Louisa her name and age, if she had been hurt, how great a time she had wandered the moors, what he could do for her; such things. To the last query, Louisa, who had been evasive or whimsical, had said, very simply, her long feathers of lashes lowered on her cheeks, "To be shown your kindness would be the sure sign of God's mercy." And to this he had responded, "Well, God is merciful, we trust." He had already helped her, creakily, into the carriage himself, while the young fat man huffed and puffed. And they drove towards Maskullance Manor, for the old man was Lord Maskullance, and the young, his nephew. They had been in the nearest town on the business of money, of which there was a great deal. And Louisa had followed this meaty matter with the daintiness of a spun-sugar dessert.

Presently they entered the park and so reached the manor in sheets of rain. Louisa beheld the grounds and house with the calm pleasure of one who has seen nothing, been nowhere, expects everything, and has little imagination.

The carriage was attended to, and the two men and Louisa, passed into the house under the huge black umbrellas of the footmen.

Here, below an ornate staircase, on a floor like a chess-board, stood a large sable piece, with plumes of white hair, shiny eye-glasses, and a mysterious large lump in one cheek.

Louisa detected instantly another antagonist: She could not see his eyes.

"Behold, my faithful retainer, Mr. Sheepshead," said old Lord Maskullance with a smile.

"My Lord," said Mr. Sheepshead, and bowed—the lump equally mysteriously disappeared. He was both steward and butler and had served the family since Lord Maskullance and he were children. He was one of those servants who twine like supportive weeds about the structure of a house. Disturb them and the bricks collapse. And this too Louisa sensed, without knowing anything about it.

"Sheepshead, we met a lady called Louisa in the meads," went on his lordship. "We must treat her carefully, and perhaps there will be three wishes for all of us."

"My Lord. Miss Louisa."

"Hrughch," hawked Bleston.

They moved from the chequered hall into a side parlour of some magnificence. Again, there were no slabs of gold or swags of jewels, but a plushy lustre, velvet and cut glass, and against the dark day, in lily-like lamps, a blue-yellow phosphorous burned that Louisa's erstwhile limited reading gave her suppose was gas-light.

In the manor parlour the whole tribe had assembled, as if on purpose.

By a shining table with a glowing pomander of fruit upon it, sat Lord Maskullance's elderly unwed sister, Millicent, a spike of a woman clad in mauve. She had been embroidering, for she believed that work of an unfortunate nature was found for idle hands, not realizing how much less appetizing work may be found by a certain sort of idle mind.

At another table inlaid with mosaics sat the widowed younger sister of Lord Maskullance, Agathena, who had been playing Snatch with fifty two cards and her offspring, Maud. Agathena and Maud were that phenomenon, a mother and daughter who look almost exactly alike, but also they were both similar to an animal, which in this case was a rather pretty pig.

Maud's younger brother, Georgie, slumped before the hearth

reading a newspaper. He was only like his mother and sister in the pig department, although he bore a slight likeness to his elder brother Bleston.

Despite the fact no jewels hung from the ceiling or were pressed into the walls, Louisa was glad to see that everyone in the room had been lightly sprinkled with them.

The company looked up when she came in; Lord Maskullance had opened the door for her. Agathena was the only one to exclaim. But Bleston, pushing in at Louisa's back, took up the cry.

"Exactly, mother. What do you think of it? Uncle saw this young woman on the moor, and, ain't I damned, insisted she be brought here, in her rags and soaked with rain as she is."

Since they were all the dependents of Lord Maskullance, not one of them could find fault with his act, only with his judgement. And this they prepared to do.

"Who ever is she?" asked Agathena.

"Some vagabond?" asked Millicent. "Surely not."

"She's dripping on the carpet," said Maud.

"Dashed odd," contributed Georgie.

It came to Louisa, as she demurely scanned them, that her aunt's predictions, again, were not entirely accurate. Only one of these people had so far taken her bait. But at least, judging the social strata of the house faultlessly from her lessons, Louisa knew he was the right one.

"Louisa," said Lord Maskullance now, in gentle, obdurate tones, "is my guest. She has suffered unhappiness, which to a lady of her breeding," (Louisa saw as he said this that he did not really credit it, and that it did not bother him) "as we know, is more cruel than to any woman of the common order. She is not to be interrogated. She is not to be harried. She shall be my ward. I've never had a ward, only the parcel of you. Of course, I'm delighted to have you all here with me, you add an indescribable sparkle to my declining years. But I see no

17

reason why one more shouldn't shelter beneath my wing."

"Oh, uncle," said Maud archly, "and I thought I was your favourite."

"Ever and always, dear Maud. But Louisa doesn't need to be my favourite. Louisa simply is. Are you not, my dear?"

Louisa dipped her green-sherry eyes. Lord Maskullance laughed aloud in pleasure. Louisa said, "You're very kind. More kind than one in my position could hope for. I trust I won't be a burden to the house."

Hearing her trained voice, the others started. They had been trusting she would utter the notes of a fish-wife. Louisa knew, just as she knew his lordship was not fooled and did not mind, that the rest of them, even the surly Bleston, had swallowed her lie. They thought her one of themselves, though demoralized, outcast, and badly-clad. A hunger lit them like the gas-jets to turn her inside out.

"We must all," said Lord Maskullance, "remember the Princess and the Pea."

Georgie said, "Eh?"

"And now," said Lord Maskullance, "one of the maids shall take Louisa to the Blue Room."

"But that is the room—" cried Millicent, appalled, "that was kept for your bride!"

"And as we know, I have never taken one and am now too old to think of taking one. But the room's fresh and pretty. Let it be used. Let Louisa have it."

Louisa entered into the Blue Room as a butterfly enters an iris. It was hers by right. It was what she had always waited for. Lovelier by far than the drawings in the books. The curtains were of royal blue velvet and the canopy of the bed. There were filmy intermediary curtains with hyacinth blue bows. (The windows overlooked the lawn and lake.) The carpet was cream and woven with gigantic indigo violets and violet roses. There were bluebirds on the wall-paper. The candles and gas-lamps were in holders of white and cerulean china trimmed with gold. The basin and ewer were like lapis lazuli. The clock *was* lapis lazuli.

On the bed were pillows edged with streamlets of lace. On the counterpane were embroidered cornflowers.

Despite the restraint in the matter of gold, Louisa was philosophical. Perhaps gold had gone out of fashion.

Soon after she had possessed the room, clothes began to arrive. Where they came from who knew? Perhaps a trousseau had been got up too for the mooted non-materializing bride. There were numerous gowns for every time of day, all of which Louisa recognized correctly, undergarments and accompanying linen. There were gloves and hats, scarves and sashes, shoes and umbrellas. Last came a casket—of gold. Inside was a pearl bracelet, a bracelet of sapphires, a broach with another sapphire, and a golden necklace hung with three pendant emeralds.

Louisa was not taken aback.

Having bathed in an adjacent chamber with blue and pink lights in the windows, Louisa summoned the maid who had been allotted to her—a solid creature called Prudent—and was dressed for dinner.

A vision then went down, in a cucumber evening creation, hair astonishingly built into a Roman mode, (Prudent was also handy) and garlanded by the emeralds, whose inclusions had drawn raptures from prince and pauper alike for more than one hundred years.

"Ah!" screamed Maud, Millicent and Agathena in a harmonizing chord. Maud added, "That's grandmother's necklace!"

"And one day it will be yours, dear Maud," said Lord Maskullance in the most soothing and gentlemanly of tones. "Till then, permit Louisa to borrow it."

And Louisa knew, without having the words to describe his sadism, that the one who loved her was also canny and cruel. She was to be his vengeance on this pack who had so bored him.

She peeled away the pale fingers of her gloves and set about the demonstration of her perfect table manners. They were much better than Maud's, far far better than Bleston and Georgie's.

How easy it was, the world. All she must do now was to persuade his lordship to wed her, and surely he was halfway there already? The rest was violence.

There was an impediment.

Louisa could not have guessed. The books omitted speaking of such things.

Old Lord Maskullance was not, and never had been, inclined to ladies. Which was not to say he was not ready to fall madly, *aesthetically* in love with them. He had been almost ceaselessly infatuated in his youth, now with this famous beauty, now with that. He would write them poems, he would speak of the heaven-softness of their hair, the liquid clarity of their eyes, and the alabaster of their complexions. He would send gifts, he would seek their company. He would sit beneath their windows night-long, in moon-beam and rain storm. But take them to wife he would not. At length his measure was gaged. No one any more expected marriage of him, and several pleasant and civilized liaisons occurred, after which the lady in question might pass on, physically quite unsullied, but considerably advanced in the financial way. His family, especially his sisters Millicent and Agathena, had never faced up to his lordship's preference. They had manufactured the formula of embitterment, a youthful broken heart. Latterly, Bleston and Georgie took care that any sniggering went on *sotto voce*.

In old age Lord Maskullance had seemed to give over all his former practices. He led a blameless existence with his batch of relatives, now the sole beneficiaries of his delightful will, merely accruing wealth innocently, as a matter of course. Truly nothing had stirred him but controlled exasperation and a caustic dislike for more than twenty years. Then Louisa flamed upon his sight. Perhaps now too old to be aroused in the other way, or at least to have any hope of indulgence, his lordship responded to Louisa as the jaded desensitized palate which suddenly discerns a taste.

There was too the added attraction of using her to provoke his ghastly tribe.

But marry her—never. There were dreadful tales of young wives who clambered into bed with an elderly spouse, insisting upon their rights. It was not to be risked. Besides, he was too fastidious to live out such untruth. Louisa should fill the silver niche of his dream, the last of her kind, as perhaps he was the last of his.

The days of Maskullance Manor passed, marked out by the chimes of clocks, ringing of servants' bells, the dinner gong, and the continuous eerie shriek of the peacocks. "I'd shoot the damn things," said Bleston whenever he heard them. His mother frivolously laughed, perhaps not believing him, or not caring. Maud was unfavourable. Peacocks were not game birds. One might massacre pheasants, bludgeon cattle and lambs, destroy difficult horses, skin bears, ride down foxes, but very young kittens, singing canaries, peacocks and so on, had been given another function, that of entertainment, by God.

One day all this would be theirs. Would Bleston then go out with his gun, even as Georgie rode amok from the stables?

Now and then Maud walked to the village, accompanied by a maid. She seldom returned with anything. Some young labourers were building a cottage, and Maud would pause to watch.

Millicent embroidered her samplers. *He seeth all.* She was thinking not of God, but that Alice might have been unwise with the youngest footman. Alice must be watched. To Millicent a peacock was of no interest. People interested her. She feared for them, their morals, their foolishness upon the primrose path. She kept a close eye on Louisa. She tried to draw Louisa out. But Louisa was reticent. Flamboyantly so. "I can say nothing. It would be painful to me, and to you, madam, to hear." Georgie was also inclined to watch Louisa. Millicent considered what might happen there. Louisa was a lady, albeit a fallen one (how had she fallen?). What would Georgie do? Millicent viciously stitched an eye into a pansy.

She had never seemed to notice Maud's jaunts to cottages, or her eying of two or three of the younger footmen.

Agathena had tried to befriend Louisa. Agathena had played cards with Louisa—book-educated in such games, Louisa invariably won. Agathena spared Louisa reminiscences and confessions of her own past, in the hopes of eliciting a response. "Well, that's enough of me. Now what of you?" "I can say nothing," said Louisa. "Don't press me." "One must confide," said Agathena. "Oh, a terrible headache has come on," said Louisa, rising up with her lace handkerchief at her marble brow and drifting out.

Maud spurned—if it is possible to spurn that which does not care—Louisa, as Bleston did. (Of course Maud had her labourers and footmen to interest her.) To Georgie Maud said severely, "Don't ogle her, Georgie. She's a minx." For she was modern and spoke her mind. Also one that doeth, knoweth that others do.

"Ogle who?" asked Georgie, pretending to be as stupid as he truly was.

Sheepshead hovered faultlessly through the house. Now one cheek bulged, now the other—toothache? A migratory boil?

So the days and nights passed, with their sidling insinuations, lumps, stares and rasps. And in his chair Lord Maskullance looked on, gazing at everything as if at a play. Sometimes he would—as when Louisa left with her headache—openly applaud.

In the evenings, when Maud bad-temperedly thumped at the piano forte, Louisa would dance alone across the chequered floor, measures learned by rote in the cottage where now frogs might feed, if they would, upon her aunt. Gossamer was Louisa, thistledown, with the waist of a snake.

The stars chimed, the warning bells of envy and malice rang, there were shrieks in closed minds, and the occasional gong of lust in Georgie's uncomely body.

But what of Louisa? Under her silk and satin hide, what did she think of it? She thought, of course, it went too slowly. By now the old man should have succumbed, the nuptial been arranged. As his wife, she would enter the waiting-room of his treasury. A Blue Chamber, a chest of clothes, three emeralds were appetizing, but not enough. He was so old. Every morning she wondered if he would descend. And if he did not, there were these others, who would drive her out at once.

Louisa entered the breakfast room.

"My Lord, I must speak to you—alone."

His lordship glowed. Millicent and Bleston, the only other early risers, glared.

None would be sorry to leave the breakfast. The excellence of meals had fallen off. The green-faced skinny cook, Mrs. Crampp, had recently seemed to be worrying over something and the culinary arrangements suffered.

"We'll take a stroll under the grape pergola," said Lord Maskullance and took Louisa on his arm away into the knot garden. "Eyes will soon be everywhere," he told her. "Do you really wish to unburden yourself?"

"No," said Louisa, departing from the books, "only to ask you why you don't marry me?"

"Hah!" exclaimed Lord Maskullance, with genuine glee.

"I've been here almost a month."

"And so you have. Don't you suppose I'm a trifle ancient for a bridegroom?"

"Naturally," said Louisa. "But it doesn't hinder me."

"Why not?"

"Because," and here Louisa went back to the books, "lacking your protection, what will become of me?"

"I think you mean if I should die."

Louisa lowered her lashes. "Don't speak of it. It upsets me so. What's that whistling? Is it some giant bird?"

"No cause for alarm. Sheepshead is checking the coverts. He has a police whistle which he blows to call the keepers to where he is. On the other matter," went on Lord Maskullance, "I have an idea of what to do. You shall become my legal ward and be popped into my will. I can't promise very much, my dear girl, since most of it must go to the greedy vultures, all of whom are now about you will notice through his hedge, and searching the topiary and the peach arbour to find us. However, there is the added attraction to my will that if any of them should perish, the spoils will then be divided among the remaining persons, whose number will have come to include yourself."

"How could they perish?" asked Louisa. "How loud Sheepshead's whistle is!"

"Bleston might give in to an apoplexy. Note his fat red form and the amount of brandy he consumes. Georgie might be thrown, he treats my horses abominably and they'd love to kill him. The women are probably indestructible."

Louisa smiled. In a way that could not find out and did not need words, she now sensed a confederate of no mean proportion. Did his lordship know it himself? At that moment, as she thanked him for his goodness in the matter of the will, she beheld Mr. Sheepshead placing himself unsuitably behind a statue of Venus. Mr. Sheepshead's glasses shone. Between his lips shone the whistle. They were like the eyes and beak of some dreadful bug. Clearly he had heard everything.

"Sheepshead I don't grudge," said Lord Maskullance. "His share of my estate has been well-earned."

Sheepshead slipped away among the yew hedges and presently collided there with Agathena.

On the ground below Venus lay some of Mr. Sheepshead's snuff, spilled in a brown patch.

"His only vice," remarked Lord Maskullance with disapproving admiration. "Except perhaps," he added, "his passion for humbugs."

t caused upheaval and then silence. It was like a thunderclap followed by a pause before the angels speak. The wardship and the alteration to the will.

Lawyers went back and forth. Sheafs of paper spread across the library's mahogany table, the great globe of the whole world pushed to one side.

Each member of his family attempted to advise Lord Maskullance against it. Such a little *little* amount, but why should this stray have it?

"She charms me," said Lord Maskullance with utter truth. How cruel truth so often is. She charmed, they did not.

They sulked. They muttered. Like Shakespearian villains they skulked in corridors and bushes, listened at doors and learned only what they already knew.

How he must have enjoyed it. He smiled on them almost with love. Then took Louisa's arm and walked about the gardens and the park.

"Are you secure now, Louisa?" Louisa gave him one of his own early roses. "Never a rose without a thorn," he said.

"Should you *like*," she said, for she had learnt now to speak beyond the books, with him, "a rose without a thorn?"

*   *   *

25

ouisa sat at luncheon in Maskullance Manor, glancing about her under her shade-lashes, wondering simply, *Who shall be first?* From a small drawer in the Blue Room, a drawer having blue enamel butterflies upon it, she had taken out a lace handkerchief in which was wrapped her sole memento of the cottage on the mire and of her now skeletal aunt. The phial of clear liquid.

As if pulling the petals of a flower, she looked them over. This one, *that* one. That one, *this* one. Which would be best, most apt? For Louisa was an artist in her own way. She liked symmetry and patterns. Perhaps she should find some means to make them draw lots . . . whoever raised their knife the next? No, it was his lordship, and his lordship must be left until the last—

Georgie got up, thrusting back his chair and Sheepshead who was behind him. Sheepshead stepped away decorously, unruffled, only the humbug abruptly evident in one cheek. Georgie went to the sideboard.

"This food is foul. I'll take some brandy, uncle, if you don't mind."

"Please do," said Lord Maskullance. "Perhaps Bleston has left you some."

Bleston grunted.

Georgie, glass filled, came by Louisa and paused to admonish her. "Try to eat more, old girl. Or you won't grow up big and strong like Maudie."

Maud clucked with annoyance, and Georgie slipped one hand down upon Louisa's knee. The movement was swift and barely to be noticed; he seemed to have adjusted her napkin. He had just drawn for himself the relevant straw.

Louisa gave him one ravished glance. It was an action as swift as his own. Georgie reddened and licked his lips.

After luncheon, Georgie made a great to do about going out to the stables.

"Should you ride after all that brandy?" inquired his solicitous mother, to whose eyes perhaps he and Bleston were beautiful and virtuous.

"Yes, mother. Of course I should. Give that grey thing a taste of my crop." And he winked, for Lord Maskullance had left the dining chamber.

After Georgie was departed, the ladies retired to their rooms to rest, a chronic post-luncheon procedure.

Louisa did not retire.

Soon she was on the beech walk which led from the stables to the park. She moved slowly, twirling her parasol, and in a few minutes Georgie rode up on the grey gelding, which as usual was flinching beneath him and rolling its eyes.

"See how it obeys," said Georgie, "eh, Louisa? It's getting to know who's master."

"It's true you're masterful, sir."

"A horse is one thing. A pretty woman another."

Louisa had very few emotions of her own; the swamp had not inclined her to grow them. Of sex she knew next to nothing, only its stylized symbols and the ardour of gentlemen, from her books. She therefore dealt with Georgie after their manner, in the mode of a well-bred flirt. But Georgie liked that.

When Louisa dropped her lace handkerchief on the ground: "Oh I say," said Georgie and started to dismount. "Stand you brute. *Stand* I say, or do you want correction?" The horse stood like a stone, and Georgie plumped down and retrieved the handkerchief. He gave it to Louisa.

"For your gallantry you must have my favour, sir."

"A kiss?" asked Georgie hopefully, meaning by this naughty slightness things far steamier, gropings and liftings, a promise for the dark.

"First," said Louisa, "a rose. And on the rose I will place two drops of this."

27

"Why, what is it?" chortled Georgie.

"A love potion."

"What, you want my love, do you?"

Louisa lowered her eyes and held out to him the flower, on which now reposed two clear drops from the glass phial.

"I see you set no store by magic," said Louisa. "But I warn you. Touch the dew to your lips, and you're lost to me."

"Lost, am I? Think I daren't? What a wench it is." And Georgie touched the rose and its two drops to his lips, licked them off. Swallowed them. "And now—a kiss!"

"First let me see you ride," said Louisa. "Just one canter across the lawn. I dearly like to see a gentleman on a horse. Then come back, sir knight, and claim your reward."

"Tally ho!" yelled Georgie. "I believe your potion works. I never smelled a rose so sweet!" And flinging his lumpen self back aloft, he took the horse by storm, kicking in the spurs and slashing it across the neck with his crop. Off it went like a ball bursting from a cannon. They ran straight at the lawn and tore along the grass beneath the mullioned windows of the house.

Louisa stood in the shadows of the beech walk. There was no one else in sight. She had stopped twirling her parasol.

Georgie gave a hoarse loud cough.

Then, like a clown in a circus, he rose from the stirrups up into the air and executed, over the rump of the horse, one perfect somersault. By the time he came down, the grey was gone from under him, had bolted in a panic to be free of Georgie, straight across the park towards the lake. Louisa did not wait for more. She hastened along the walk, up some steps, and through a side door of the house.

Here in a passage she met suddenly with Sheepshead.

"I was just about to go into the garden, Sheepshead, when I remembered I'd left my gloves behind."

"I shall send one of the maids to fetch them, Miss Louisa."

Louisa waited in an island of the house, by a polished table with roses upon it. She thought of Georgie in the grass and the horse dashing across the park. Her gloves, removed behind her back and thrust into the sash of her dress, beat with two little cheerful hearts against her serpent waist. Things could not have gone much better. Sheepshead had only been an extra test of her quickness.

The maid came with some gloves. As Louisa took them, a wild shouting began on the lawn beyond the beech walk. Georgie had been thrown, and his spine was broken. Georgie was no more.

The funeral of Georgie was lavish. Black plumed black horses pulled the hearse, and all the relative carriages. Georgie in his box was not able to beat these animals, and they moved at a slow and sombre pace. At the graveside Agathena leant on Bleston; she wept and he scowled. The curate conducted the service dramatically. He told them all how they had adored Georgie, how everyone had worshipped him, how he would be missed. Millicent dabbed her lips but not her eyes. White-faced, Maud managed a tear.

In the carriage returning to the manor, utter silence presided over Agathena's sobs.

"Mother, don't take on so," complained Bleston, perhaps afraid of rheumatism in his wet shoulder.

"Not take on—your only brother dead—dead—"

Lord Maskullance had not attended the funeral. "Forgive me," he had said, "I feel too frail to witness the burial of one so young."

The funeral baked meats were uneatable.

In the house the days now plodded like the black horses, having nothing to make them go. It was not possible to do anything. To play the piano or cards did not show respect. One might only sit and cry, or sit and read some holy tract for consolation. Millicent embroidered: *The lamb is taken unto God.* Georgie, the lamb.

Curbing a desire to abscond to the Blue Room and play there with her trinkets and toys, Louisa stationed herself in the parlour. After all, she would have to get used to these funerals. And her funeral clothes were of the very best, elegant black silk, muslin; black suited Louisa, with her hair already in mourning, in contrast to her eyes and skin.

Louisa watched, hour by hour.

Who should be next?

One afternoon Maud stood on the terrace like a black dumpling, gazing out across the lawn towards the lake. She might have been reliving in memory Georgie's tragic end. Nevertheless, a young man, presumably one of the newer gardeners, was scrabbling about in a border of the lawn. He was a strong young fellow, in dreadful shapeless clothes, and as he toiled the sun lit up his red hair.

Maud was modern. She said outright to Louisa, "A fine fellow. Sturdy peasant stock."

From her books Louisa understood the social levels must not mingle, and what savage scandals had been hinted of when they did.

"Take care," said Louisa.

"What? Impudence. Why should I?"

"That young man," said Louisa into Maud's unshell-like ear, "often looks at you with hot eyes. I've seen him. I have thought of telling Lord Maskullance—"

"Don't dare," cried Maud. She bridled and flushed a rosy beetroot. "Does he? Look at me?"

"Sometimes," improvised Louisa, "he hides in the bushes when you walk about the park. Once—I hardly dare repeat it—I heard him growl like a dog."

Maud was all of a flummox. She did not know what to do

with herself. She dithered and skipped about the terrace, fanning herself with her black fan, on which was painted a funeral wreath. And in the midst of all this, the young gardener, innocently, raised his copper head from the border, and behind Maud's back Louisa lifted her hand and vigorously waved. The gardener *stared*.

"See. He's staring at you this minute."

"Oh whatever shall I do?"

"We must go in," experimented Louisa.

"No. That would be to make too much of it. After all, these are modern times. A cat may look at a king."

"But not growl."

"Yes, I'd forgotten the . . . growl."

"Better to go in," wheedled Louisa.

"No, I'll best him, the saucy fellow." And Maud took Louisa's arm by force. "We shall cross the lawn. We shall go by the border. See if he brazens a look at me then."

Arm in arm, they rushed over the grass—Maud set the pace. The gardener, beholding the gallop, looked nervous and buried himself in the rhododendrons.

"I'm shocked," said Maud when they reached the lake. "To ogle me at such a time, when I'm in mourning."

"But it does suit you so, the black."

"Yes awful isn't it." Maud warmed to Louisa all at once. For a moment, at the start, Maud had been intrigued by Louisa. Perhaps there was something to her after all. They were both girls, (Maud a girl over thirty) pretty and free of heart, bound by the dictates of their elders and now—united in sorrow, Louisa's dread secret and Maud's untimely loss. "Lady Findrangle refused to come out of mourning for her husband, you know, the black suited her so well." Maud glanced back at the border. The gardener had fled. "A coward."

"Or perhaps it may be worse," said Louisa. "Perhaps he has

dared to fall in love with you."

Maud digested this. It was possible . . .

"Dear Louisa, you must be my confidante. I'm not sure what I should do. The poor boy—He'd pulled up half the flowers in his nervousness."

"Perhaps not always so poor," said Louisa thoughtfully. "It seems the other older gardeners consider him something of a protégé of his lordship's. One day, Lord Maskullance is supposed to have said, that young man may be designing half the great gardens in the country."

Maud sat bold upright. She was a pig dreaming of being the scandalous wife of the famous gardener and genius who designed half the great gardens in the country. She had once or twice had fancies of running off with a footman, but luckily they resisted their hopes, not able to bring themselves to speak to her of their feelings. Thus she had been spared agonizing decisions of flight and loss. This, though, was different. It was all the rage. So many society beauties had done it—at least in books—that it was almost *fashionable.*

"I have a confession," said Louisa. "The gardener asked me yesterday to bring a letter to you, and I refused."

"Refused!"

"Shall I seek him out and accept the letter on your behalf?"

"Certainly not. Oh Louisa! Certainly."

"What a joy it is," said Louisa, "to see the colour in your cheeks again."

Colour there surely was. Maud rose like a funereal lobster and hurried towards the house.

On her own journey there, Louisa caught sight of another red thing, which was curiously flapping above the wall of the kitchen garden—perhaps some kind of strange large bird, maybe an escaped parrot. She did not bother with it, but went to her room, and on a scrap of paper ripped from the back of a book of poems, she penned a gross little note in the awful penmanship of the mire. Her aunt had dealt only in surfaces—easily worthy of an unlettered gardener. *Dearist,* it said, *I have somethink to speek to you off, that is onli for yor owne dear ears.*

It went on to entreat Maud to go out after the dinner hour and down to the lake. There among the trees hearts should be opened wide.

Louisa did not search out Maud. Louisa waited patiently, as was her wont between deeds, until Maud, unable to contain herself, came knocking on the Blue Room door.

"I have it," said Louisa, "but, oh, should I—"

"Give it here!" roared Maud, and she grasped the paper. She read the missive with slight unease. "What awful spelling. But there, a rough diamond. Does he need to spell in order to work miracles amid the flowers?"

"Will you go?" asked Louisa, aghast,

"I must."

"Then, let me advise you, dear Maud. This evening, before the others, refuse your dinner, make a great display of grief."

"What for?" inquired Maud.

"For your brother Georgie."

"Oh, yes. Georgie."

"Show your sadness," said Louisa, "as, until now, you've hidden your tears, so bravely, to comfort your mother and aunt."

Maud pondered this and managed to add a little moisture to the end of her nose. She wiped it. "Yes."

"Then go up to your room. Say you must be left alone with your despair. They'll honour this. You can slip out very simply. I'll accompany you for safety to the lake and leave you there. With him."

"Louisa you're a true friend. I won't forget your sympathy." They embraced. After a moment Maud said cautiously, "Is it absolutely necessary, do you think, that I refuse to eat? I grow

33

faint very quickly if I omit a meal. Even one of Mrs. Crampp's ghastly dinners."

"I'll bring food for you to the lake."

"Ah, Louisa!"

As Louisa let Maud from her door, they saw Sheepshead passing at the end of a passage.

"Can he have overheard?" asked Maud.

"I don't believe so," said Louisa. "He's old. His hearing is probably impaired."

"Uncle's isn't."

"Lord Maskullance is unusual. But we must be extra careful. Here, let me destroy the letter."

When Maud was gone, Louisa dismissed Sheepshead from her brain. She doubted he had listened at the door—her acute instincts would have warned her. He was only troublous in being always in the right place at the wrong time.

That evening Maud gave a performance of which the greatest actresses of her day might have been envious. She scorned all food, she wept and screamed, squeezing water from her eyes by the sheer volume of her shrieks. How she had loved Georgie, peerless, matchless Georgie, cut down in his prime. Remaining mother and brother could never make up his sum. Oh she recalled his childhood, his scrapes, how he had come to her with his childish scratches, and when the keeper's ferrets had set on him. And now Georgie was gone, what was life worth? What did she care?

Dumbfounded by her outburst, no one argued. Maud tossed a small crystal vase at a wall. It shattered near Sheepshead's left cheek and he moved aside.

"Leave me alone," said Maud, (no one had gone near her) "let me go to my room and exhaust myself in misery."

They did so, only glad she had vacated the dining room.

Soon Louisa rose with a headache—they could quite credit she had it tonight. She asked for provisions on a tray.

Later, in the moonless dark, two women in black crept down to the lakeside, disturbing the feeding ducks.

"Is he here yet? Good, there's time to eat that pie. Oh Louisa, old Crampp's improved! How wonderful this tastes—I never tasted a pie so—" and Maud, having devoured also in her haste one single drop from the glass phial, closed her eyes and fell, with a hefty plop, into the lake.

The ducks scurried from her impact, but presently returned, encouraged that she did not come up again.

Louisa retraced her silent steps to the house. She met no one; even the parrot was gone from the kitchen garden. When once she thought she heard a whistle she realized this was foolish. She passed into her Blue Room and a dreamless slumber. From which insane cries aroused her early the next morning, in time to see, from her windows, the drowned body of Maud being fished from the lake.

They're dwindling, Louisa," said Lord Maskullance, as they strolled about the apple orchard.

"They seem so healthy. Some are even turning pink."

"Not the apples, Louisa."

She met his eyes for three angelic seconds. "Whom, then?"

"The dependents of my blood."

"Your lordship's bereavement is barely to be supported."

"Yet, as you see, I do."

The funeral had been quiet, quieter than the first. Maud's suicide—rather her accident, stumbling and falling into the lake—was no longer spoken of.

As Lord Maskullance and Louisa passed among the apples, Louisa saw Sheepshead moving stealthily after them, behind the trees.

"Does he often follow you?" inquired Louisa.

Lord Maskullance did not glance about. "A recent obsession."

"Has he," Louisa paused, discreetly, "informed you of its cause?"

"Not at all. Perhaps a fascination with yourself."

Louisa considered. On the evening when she left Maud in the lake, had glasses glinted starlight from the bushes? If Sheepshead had been a witness to the deed, surely he must have spoken out.

"Your lordship is very attached to Sheepshead," said Louisa.

"I remember him from my boyhood," said Lord Maskullance.

"And for his service, you remember him in your will."

"Quite so."

They walked across the grass and came upon a View, the sweep of Maskullance Park, its oaks, its meadows, and beyond them the wilderness of the moor, that sea of primeval chaos which, hidden or not, surrounded everything.

"Do you love your Mr. Sheepshead very dearly?" asked Louisa, with innocent tenderness.

"I love only you," said Lord Maskullance.

"He seems frail," said Louisa.

"As are we all."

He had not attended Maud's funeral. It was too distressing for his old bones.

Now he smiled on the lovely thing he had brought into his house.

An apple dropped before its time. Mr. Sheepshead slunk behind a tree, cheek bulging.

*　　*　　*

hey were four at luncheon.

"Someone must speak to Crampp," declared Mill-cent, plying herself with an indigestion remedy. "I'm in agonies after these appalling repasts."

"Filthy muck," agreed Bleston. "I'll dine at the inn, uncle."

"Of course, Bleston," replied Lord Maskullance. "What luck for me, the impaired digestion and failure of the sense of taste inherent in old age spare me any special distress at Mrs. Cramp's new diet."

Agathena kept to her room. She ate from trays and wept, keeping the laundry also busy with her reams of handkerchiefs.

Louisa ate daintily and thoroughly. She had been brought up on the messes of the mire.

Behind the chairs patrolled the impeccable Sheepshead. His cheeks did not bulge; Louisa, by offhand questionings of Prudent and a footman, knew why. Mr. Sheepshead was out of both humbugs and snuff. He must today go down into the village to supply himself.

It was a sunny, ripening afternoon. Beyond the park gates, the moor burned up its bracken goldenly. Louisa passed between the smouldered slopes, staying wisely on the path, which in parts was hemmed by standing stones. She had come this way but once before, in the carriage and the rain.

The late summer village was as she remembered it, and she had no trouble in locating the apposite shop with its displays of pipes in one window and, in the other, black liquorice in jars and beetle-like mounds of humbugs.

In sailed Louisa, who for the occasion had put on her plainest dress and shadowed her face with a vast straw hat.

"I be yeer for mey pappy's bag o' umbugs," said Louisa, in a very bad rendition of the local dialect.

"Humbugs, miss. And surely I knows another gentleman that be partial to them."

Louisa ordered an enormous quantity, paid for them with coins extracted now and then from Prudent, and next sent the shop-keeper on a search for some other sweetmeat. During his absence Louisa administered a single drop from her phial to one solitary humbug. It would wait its turn, but its turn would come.

"I hope as how," said the tobacconist, reappearing to Louisa without the second sweet, "you haven't strayed alone across the moor?"

"Perhaps not," said Louisa, in rather the wrong voice.

"For you'll not have heard the great gun, maybe. A lunatic's got out of the asylum and be at large, desperate and dangerous. And he's been gone some time, they do say, and only just come to the notice."

"I see my companion on the street," said Louisa and floated from the shop. Outside she swiftly vanished along an alley between the butcher's and the inn. In vain did the tobacconist come to his door with the enormous bag of humbugs.

When Mr. Sheepshead arrived, these lost sweets would be presented to him. It would be irresistible to the tobacconist and sweetseller, who was apparently deferential to all the servants from the manor and to (said Prudent) the butler-steward particularly, to offer him gratis his favourite suck.

Louisa returned to the manor and, on the way, beholding the figure of Sheepshead up the path, she took refuge, rather in his own way, behind a suitable standing stone. He did not seem to notice her and stepped on towards the village.

Recrossing the manor grounds, Louisa again caught sight of a curious red phenomenon atop the kitchen garden wall. It was not a red parrot.

Louisa stole to the small door in the wall, and easing it open, peeped into the garden. Amid the salad, mounted on a garden seat, was the thin green cook Mrs. Crampp, waving earnestly aloft a pair of scarlet flannelette bloomers.

Without changing expression Louisa withdrew from the door and restored herself to the house, there to await the eventual sad tidings of Mr. Sheepshead's demise.

Prudent relayed the awful news to Louisa as she was dressing her in black watered silk for dinner.

"And poor Mr. Sheepshead goes to the door of the shop, and what should he see but his old friend stretched out on the liquorice chews."

The cheery tobacconist had, it seemed, suffered from a sudden fatal seizure of the heart. It transpired it was a peaceful end, nevertheless, for the dead man had even a smile on his face, and round him on the ground were strewn the contents of a bag of humbugs he had been happily consuming. He was very fond of them. Fonder even than poor Mr. Sheepshead.

"I shall wear the sapphires," said Louisa.

She was philosophical. She would not be discouraged.

The dinner though was one of the worst so far experienced. Millicent declined it and swallowed instead her mixture. Bleston was absent. Lord Maskullance sat in his chair, hooded eyes beaming with definite cruelty on his sparse fellow diners.

Sheepshead presided flat-cheeked behind the chairs. He gave no sign of any shock, let alone any perturbation.

"Tell Mrs. Crampp," said Lord Maskullance, "she has to-night surpassed herself."

After she had retired, and while she was having her evening communion with her mirror, a procedure sometimes lasting two or three hours, Louisa heard an odd rustling beneath her windows. Only the lamp before the mirror was lit. Going to the curtains, she pulled them slightly aside and gazed down into the shrubbery. Perhaps something moved there, or not. A faint noise, something like a bleat, rose up into the still night. Perhaps it was a wandering pheasant.

Louisa remembered the coverts and that Mr. Sheepshead was soon due to visit them again. This thought sent her to bed in a much gladdened state of mind.

heepshead moved across the park. Now and then his whistle sounded, and a keeper would leap out and debate with him. Louisa followed, a slender black muslin shape. In a basket on her arm reposed a few plucked flowers, her excuse for persistence. Occasionally she was assisted by finding flowers already pulled up at their roots.

Now and then things rustled in the undergrowth. Louisa was put in mind of large dogs crawling on their bellies. She had not realized pheasants were so large.

Sheepshead did not put down the whistle, which she had trusted he would do.

After a while, the steward-butler went back towards the house. As he reached the wall of the kitchen garden there was no flash of red.

Louisa manifested from a lilac.

"Good day, Sheepshead."

"Miss Louisa."

"I'll walk with you to the kitchen, Sheepshead. His lordship has asked me to speak to Mrs. Crampp."

"Indeed, miss."

"Hasn't it come to your notice, Sheepshead, how peculiarly Mrs. Crampp is behaving?"

"Indeed not, miss."

The whistle hung from a leather thong on Sheepshead's breast. It shone in the sunlight. How many times it had entered between Sheepshead's lips. Certain as a humbug.

They passed through a door into the cavern of the kitchen.

About the room, characterized already with steaming pots, and with the elements of meat and greens soon to be ruined, scullery maids and skivvies stood aghast. And at the scrubbed table, her hands in bunches of mint and onions and, strangely, chrysanthemums, Mrs. Crampp, onion-green, looked at Louisa like a soul in limbo. "Why, Miss—"

"Please don't rise, Mrs. Crampp." Louisa smiled about her benignly, book-taught on the kitchen. "All of you, continue with your duties. And you, Sheepshead, pray go on as usual."

And Sheepshead passed into the pantry and Louisa's fox's ears heard the clink of the whistle hung up on a peg.

Louisa examined the cook on the contents of luncheon.

Mrs. Crampp stammered. "I'm sorry, miss. His lordship— that is, I haven't been myself. There's been that much on my mind."

"Let me see the pantry, Mrs. Crampp," said Louisa. "I'm most interested in how you all proceed here."

Mrs. Crampp let Louisa into the pantry. Sheepshead was gone. Louisa asked for a glass of water, and Mrs. Crampp hurried away to see to it. Louisa found the whistle with no trouble, anointed it—one drop again, for a peacefulseeming death of old age—turned and took the water, looked at it lovingly, and gave it back to Mrs. Crampp.

Mrs. Crampp burst suddenly into tears. Oceans rolled from her. "Life's that unjust."

Louisa had not found it so, ultimately. She had the opportunist's amnesia. She gazed sympathetically and blankly at Mrs. Crampp.

"I'll look forward to luncheon," said Louisa.

"Oh, miss," wept the cook.

M r. Sheepshead's lost his whistle," said Prudent.

"What can you mean?"

"That police whistle of his. He hangs it in the pantry and it's gone. The boy said a magpie must have took it. But then some tarts were missing too."

Neither tarts nor whistle reappeared.

Divine providence tended to Sheepshead.

How difficult he was proving.

h miss, you shouldn't," said Prudent the following day. "Hasn't one of the ladies advised you? His lordship would—"

"His lordship lets me do as I like."

Louisa passed down again, this time via the back stairs, to the domain of the kitchen. Here the servants were about to engage in their tea. They rose in a flurry as Louisa flowed into the room. On the scrubbed board were loaves and butter, dishes of preserves, tiny sandwiches whiskered by cress, and a great walnut cake. Had Mrs. Crampp fashioned these things? It seemed unlikely, for although she sat at one end of the table, the tea pot before her, she was employed in nursing a small wooden sheep. "It was his as a boy's," she said to Louisa in a vague and hopeless yet explanatory way. "His little lamb."

"How nice, Mrs. Crampp. I trust you'll indulge me. I should like to join the below-stairs tea."

At his place, the table's opposite end, Mr. Sheepshead looked grave. Prudent said, generally, "I spoke to Miss Louisa, but—"

"Please seat yourself," interrupted Mr. Sheepshead. "Podgers, give Miss Louisa your chair."

Podgers, the youngest footman, in a dither, obliged.

Louisa sat. She was radiant.

"What a wonderful cake!"

"Alice made it," Mrs. Crampp reassured the table at large.

"How clever of Alice. May I see?" They passed the cake to Louisa. It was already accurately cut into a quantity of slices, one being twice the size of the rest.

"Whose slice is this?"

"That's for Mr. Sheepshead, madam," said Alice,

"Yes," echoed Mrs. Crampp in a ritualistic voice, like a clock ticking in spite of itself, "always the largest piece for the butler."

"Good gracious!" cried Louisa, her hand to her throat, "what can that be at the window?"

Mrs. Crampp leapt to her feet, almost oversetting the tea pot. "Is it him—Is it my Jacob?"

She plunged to the window. Two of the maids rushed to hold her back. Others faintly screamed. All eyes were on the window and the cook, even the glinting lenses of Sheepshead. All but Louisa's, as she dipped a drop of death upon the fated double slice of cake, behind the flick of a lace handkerchief. Next moment the lace was dabbing at her temples, the phial quite concealed.

"Nothing there," mourned Mrs. Crampp, sagging in the supporting arms. They bore her back to the table. Quavering, she began to pour the thick brown tea into cups.

"Whatever did you see, Miss Louisa?" said Prudent.

"It looked—" Louisa patted her heart nervously, "like an enormous red bird. I saw one the other day on the wall of the kitchen garden."

"Oh, my doomed boy," said Mrs. Crampp, "what am I to do?"

"There, there, Mrs. Crampp," said Alice hastily.

But Mrs. Crampp arose and took her toy sheep away into her parlour.

Left free, the table took on a slightly hysterical air.

"Perhaps a red parrot has got loose from some local minaginary," suggested Alice. It was obviously a lie.

Louisa was delighted by the table's determination to fool her, since it had totally obscured, it seemed to her, her own subterfuge.

The sandwiches and bread were soon consumed by the servants, hungry from overwork. All the while, Mr. Sheepshead maintained a stoical silence. Louisa chatted graciously with

Alice, Prudent and Podgers. She did not risk a direct sally at her enemy so soon to fall beneath her blade.

The moment came for the great cake.

It was passed along the table to the butler, who considered it as if from an Olympian height.

"No, I think today I must abstain."

"Oh Mr. Sheepshead," exclaimed Alice.

"Greed is a sin. I'll take this lesser slice."

Sheepshead plucked out, searing Louisa to the quick, a piece of cake several inches to the left of the prescribed slab.

The plate of the cake slid sinisterly along the table.

"Well then," said Alice, "seeing as Mr. Sheepshead doesn't, may I—"

"No, no, Alice," said one of the scullery girls, "Prudent must have it."

"No, no," said Prudent. "I can't eat all that there. I'd bust."

"Alice'll bust if she does. She's much too fat."

Alice went crimson. As the cake came to her she waved it away in injury. "I won't take any of it then, drat it."

"Hush. Before Miss Louisa," scolded Prudent. "Er, miss, could you fancy the piece? Alice is a lovely cook," she added, in solace.

"Oh, no," said Louisa, "I seldom touch cake."

"Podgers should have it then," said Prudent. "He can do with building up."

Podgers also blushed. "No, no," said Podgers, "you know I'm not much of a one for cake."

The walnut cake sat in the midst of the table, slices missing from its bulk, the great slice still glowing there, as if haloed by a mysterious and baneful light.

"I'll put it away in the pantry," said Alice. "I believe Mrs. Crampp may fancy some later."

Louisa got up; she was dissatisfied. She frowned at

Sheeps-head who had let her down and thereby exposed the innocent creatures of the kitchen, who did not track her and were not significantly included in the Maskullance will, to peril.

But Mr. Sheepshead had taken out a fresh supply of humbugs, as if to chastise her further. He put one into his cheek.

"I hope," said Louisa tartly, "your teeth don't suffer from your sweets, Sheepshead."

"My teeth are very strong, I'm pleased to say, miss."

His glass lenses blinked at her.

Louisa felt for only the second time in her life a brief flood of hatred. She would not be able to sustain so epic an emotion for long. Louisa was not a serpent, but a butterfly which stung. Nevertheless, for a few moments her thought hung palpably between them, as once, long ago, it had hung unobserved between her and her tutoring aunt. And Mr. Sheepshead twisted his thin mouth in a smile, which the humbug made ludicrous and macabre.

Something protected him, something divine or demoniac. Louisa did not perfectly believe in such things, for in her world she had found no need of them, either for help or blame. She had no conscience, required no prop. When Lord Maskullance once, as they sat in the peach arbour, referred to a demon of the Maskullances, some perhaps heraldic thing which, in any previous century was said to have protected them, neither Louisa nor his lordship gave the matter more importance than a brief discussion of the weather or the local landscape. And if from this it may be inferred that, to the pair of them, weather and landscape were also basically immaterial and unreal, that too might have been so.

However, Sheepshead was three times now saved. He was not the easy prey the others had proved to be.

She would turn from him, currently. For she did not want to waste her time. She liked to be both busy and successful.

*   *   *

45

day later, a double tragedy occurred on the moor.

A small battalion of searching policemen came upon the escaped lunatic, a wild red-headed young madman of good looks and strong physique, who lay in his shapeless institutional clothes quite close to Maskullance Park. In one hand he clutched a partly eaten piece of walnut and, in the other, a snapped leather thong. The other portion of the thong had remained with the police whistle, which the lone policeman had blown, to attract the rest of the search party. The lunatic had perhaps died of exposure, although the warm nights and the healthy state of his body made this deduction puzzling. But, since there was no mark upon him of any violence or disturbance, there seemed no other cause. A post-mortem heightened the curiosity of the case, for it ruled out even the matter of exposure. The man was fit and quite well fed from some unguessed source—the supplier of the cake. It was presently learned that other items of food had gone missing from the manor. Also, a whistle. It seemed the lunatic had always liked digging up flowers and playing with shiny things and most probably had got into the house at night and stolen the whistle in lieu of anything more attractively available.

The other, more disconcerting, part of the affair was the death of the policeman who had discovered the corpse. It seemed he had had time only to blow his summons on the handy whistle, (his own having been mislaid) when he also dropped lifeless on the earth. The policeman, too, gave no evidence either of assault or illness. He left a widow and fifteen children, but further assurance of his aggressive physical power.

The spot where the two cadavers were found quickly became ill-omened. There was talk of weird morbid gasses drifting from March Mire several miles away. Fairly soon these tales were augmented by sightings in the area of gigantic hounds, headless horses, and the ghosts of the policeman and the lunatic howling

46

and rending themselves with fingernails grown grave-long.

The tragedy on the moor had another, unexpected effect. This was upon Agathena, who emerged from her seclusion into the afternoon parlour.

"I can no longer remain here! In this den of death and iniquity."

"Indeed?" Lord Maskullance stirred in his chair. He had been watching Louisa as usual, as she played a game of Providence with an ill-humoured Bleston. The more Bleston swore, banged with the cards, and lost, the more beatific beautiful Louisa became. Millicent stitched primly at a sampler and sometimes sipped from her indigestion bottle. Although luncheon had been quite pleasant, for Mrs. Crampp had finally collapsed and the burden of the meal descended on fat Alice.

"Don't you know what goes on below-stairs?" shrieked Agathena. "That scurrilous cook—the dead lunatic was her son. Her—*unlawful* son. She's signalled to him, sheltered him. And she has fed him off our plates. And now she screams that her own food has poisoned him to death."

"Very likely," snarled Bleston. "I have you!"

"No," said Louisa. He had not.

A shower of cards hailed on the carpet.

"I will no longer stay in this nest of villainies. My children ripped from me. My only Georgie. My Maud."

"Mother," said Bleston, "control yourself."

"And *you*—no son to me!" screeched Agathena. "What have you had for me in my agony? Nothing."

"So I am to take it," said Lord Maskullance, "that you'll be going away."

"Far, far away," said Agathena.

"I'm sorry to hear it," said Lord Maskullance. He still watched Louisa, who went on playing prettily with her cards, though Bleston's were on the floor. "Where shall you go?"

47

"To my husband's cousins in the north."

"The north? A great way off."

Louisa lifted her head and looked at Agathena with the sweetest prettiest concern.

"This is a painful thing for me to say," said Lord Maskullance, smoothly, "but I grow no younger. Suppose I were to die suddenly. It would be a long and tiresome journey back to hear the will and to receive your quite considerable portion."

"What do I care for money? Don't speak of death to me over the bodies of my children."

"When," said Lord Maskullance, "do you propose to go?"

"As soon as everything can be arranged. I trust you and Bleston will assist me, as you have done in nothing else"

"Naturally. A week then."

"A week," said Agathena.

When she had quit the room, Bleston stormed to the dining room sideboard for his brandy. Millicent stitched *Virtue is triumphant*.

"Well, Louisa," said Lord Maskullance. "Only a week."

It was a fact, Agathena did not want to go north, a fearsome carriage journey of several days, to live with the dour northern cousins of her late spouse. She had wanted Lord Maskullance, Millicent, or at least her own son Bleston, to dissuade her, showing her at last some care and attention. But nothing of that had come, and the only look of concern had emanated from the stray, Louisa, with whom she had had, it must be said, some amusing hours of tattle. Even if Louisa was not herself to be drawn out, she had that marvelous facility for listening to the monologues of others so prized by everyone in another.

Perhaps of them all, Louisa, so obviously a lady, if in suspicious circumstances, Louisa had shown her friendliness.

Louisa had even come to the funerals of her children, and though she did not weep, she had had upon her a magnificent and proper solemnity, like that of a priestess who attends the sacrifice.

The door was knocked at. Agathena, who had dismissed the maid, had a second of amazed anticipation of Bleston. But then came the dulcet tone of Louisa. And though disappointed, Agathena stretched towards this visitor in the instinctive craving for likely sympathy.

Once Louisa was in the room, Agathena indulged herself in terrible tirades. She railed against her brother and sister, her son, the manor, the injustices of life. She tugged a string of pearls she wore, cried copiously, and pressed her handkerchief, as Millicent had done, to her lips rather than her eyes.

Louisa spoke little. She commiserated utterly, while managing to say no word against her benefactors. When pressed for eulogies for Georgie and Maud, she gave them in the most delicate and dramatic language, the very stuff of the best cards of condolence—from which, of course, they had been learnt.

"It's a shame you must go," said Louisa, when the outcry eventually ran down. "I'll miss you sorely."

"And I you," rampaged Agathena, believing what she spoke.

"Your sorrow's unbearable to me," said Louisa. "Oh give me your handkerchief. I have a remedy of my aunt's here, a tincture that eases bitter grief."

"How I need it." And Agathena gave to Louisa her latest handkerchief, and into the folds, so often borne to the lips, Louisa tipped a single glassy drop. "So little?"

"More would be too much."

Agathena took the handkerchief. She was on the brink of dying of grief and believed it and did not know it. She raised the handkerchief to her face, and suddenly the goodness of Louisa took her like a tempest. Its rain gushed from her eyes. Agathena lifted the handkerchief higher and crushed it not to her lips but to her streaming eyes. The lace, the drop, were engulfed.

Louisa shrank, just a very little. It was not self doubt or even fear. Yet a shrinking it was. For was this one too to be elusive?

With the impulse to remove herself from the scene of another failure, Louisa backed towards the door.

"Your pain wounds me—forgive me. I must go."

And getting out of the room, she ran to her own, where she prowled before her mirror, taking back strength from her own image, refusing Prudent entry until the gong sounded for dinner.

oming late to dinner, Louisa found Lord Maskullance, Bleston and Millicent already at table.

"You are late," chided Millicent, at once.

"I'm most sorry. I have this awful burning sensation in my throat."

"Those poor meals of Mrs. Crampp's have quite wrecked my digestion and probably yours," opined Millicent.

"I wonder if I might ask a few drops of your medicine?"

Millicent was affronted. "Have you no preparation of your own?"

"I've never suffered in this way before." Louisa pressed her fingers to her heart.

Lord Maskullance said, "Be generous, Millicent. We're told, we may go to Hell for less."

"Really!" Millicent uncorked her vial and Louisa took it humbly. "A drop, no more, in your water glass."

Louisa said to Lord Maskullance, "Might I take it in a little brandy, my Lord? I'm quite faint."

Lord Maskullance said, his eyes glittering very bright, "Sheepshead shall fetch the decanter."

"No, not at all. I'll help myself."

And Louisa went to the sideboard and poured a thimbleful of brandy and added to it a drop of Millicent's mixture, and added to Millicent's mixture from out of her sleeve another drop, much clearer and more wholesome-looking. Did any see? Sheepshead supervised the carving of the meat. A maid went round the table. A footman set down the huge tureen of soup. Bleston stuffed himself with a plate of salted anchovies. And Millicent discreetly burped.

Louisa handed the indigestion mixture to the maid to deliver back to Millicent and seated herself. She tried the brandy in a lady-like, reluctant way.

From beyond the other door, out in the vault above the chequered hall, came a freakish noise.

It was like a child's fist punching a drum. And then it was like icicles striking a glass roof. And then—

"My God! What the devil's that?" shouted Bleston jumping up.

A series of fitful sharp *brrongs* went through the air. Like imps they were, shooting arrows at a brazen target. Like tiny stones whirled inside a bell.

Everyone leant towards the door. There came a muffled rolling thud, a huge bundled bolster of sound on the stair. And then the gong gave off a bellowing clang.

Millicent rose with a squawk, clutching her mixture.

Bleston and Sheepshead ran at the door and behind them crowded the frightened maid and the footman. Lord Maskullance came last, with Louisa. Out into the hall.

Millicent breathed, "The curse of heaven is on this house." She did not leave the table where she stood. She pressed her side where her indigestion now stabbed her with knives.

At the foot of the stairs Agathena had met with the gong. She had met with it first headlong and then sideways. She lay across its surface now, her neck at a rag doll angle, with a few pearls dappled on to it. The rest, their string broken, had made the noises as they struck the carpet and the treads of the stairs, and in hitting the gong itself in the instants before Agathena did so herself. She had tumbled all the way from stair-top to bottom. They gathered about her, speechless, and from the lower stairs Alice and Podgers emerged to gather with them.

No one made a sound. Only from the dining room came the splash of Millicent at the soup.

Then his lordship spoke. "Podgers, take the trap and go for the doctor." Podgers, with a blue face, hurried off. "Too late, of course."

"She flung herself down," said Alice. "Poor madam."

"Shut up, girl," said Bleston. "The stupid woman tripped, of course."

"Blind from tears, she missed her step," Alice interpreted.

Louisa stood bathed in a silent and superb gleam, better than the brandy. The poison had not after all required insertion though the mouth. The eyes had absorbed it. True, the action was rather delayed, but so much to the good. How excellent of Agathena to be susceptible.

Lord Maskullance turned back towards the parlour.

"There'll be no need, Sheepshead, to go on with dinner."

"Excuse me," said Bleston, "there is a dashed need. I'm hungry if you ain't, uncle."

"Serve Mr. Bleston," said Lord Maskullance. His eyes settled upon Louisa. "Pale beauty stands aghast," he said, "at the vulgar ugliness of men."

It was the maid who re-entered the dining room first.

She let out a piercing shriek.

Then she ran out gesticulating and inarticulate.

Sheepshead proceeded into the room, and after a moment, called quietly, "My Lord, something else very dreadful has occurred."

They entered the room in a body, his lordship, Louisa, Bleston, Alice to the rear. After a moment Alice fainted with a loud thump. Bleston cursed. His lordship said, softly, "Use every man after his desert and who shall 'scape whipping."

Millicent had had recourse in their absence to her mixture. It worked at once to end her indigestion. She had dropped forward and into the vast tureen, submerging her head in ox-tail. They pulled her out. She was not to be revived. It seemed she had swooned and drowned, like Maud, but in the soup.

The doctor drove away. He had attended the bodies of Georgie and Maud. He attended those of Agathena and Millicent.

Perfunctory post-mortems would be carried out on the latter two corpses as on the former. Nothing fresh would be ascertained beyond the obvious. Georgie had broken his back on being thrown from a horse. Maud had drowned in the lake—a dry drowning, the heart stopping at the shock of the water, that very little fluid was in the lungs. The same was true of Millicent. The shock of the hot soup seemed to have killed her outright. Obviously Agathena had died of a snapped neck.

The perpetration of the post-mortems was a mere accession to law. Otherwise they would have been omitted. It was obvious how death had struck. One did not wish to distress a family of the Maskullance stature more than was necessary.

However, otherwise tongues wagged. The doctor's among them. Superstition and queer philosophic flight took over where suspicion might otherwise have done. Was the family cursed? Surely such a terrible flock of violent and appalling ends must stem from something? Maskullance was to be considered at least 'unlucky.'

The double funeral was of extra magnificence. Grateful for their custom, the undertaker, who had recently bought for himself a house in the nearby town, gave of his best. The ebony horses pulled the enormous hearse. Through the bones of the summer's heat the cortege drove its black uncompromising way. Earth to earth, flesh to grass. The marble mausoleum was built up over them, as if they cared. Louisa went in a carriage to place the fresh bright flowers of summer's end upon the door-step. All who saw her were charmed. They had forgotten no one knew who she was. She was the ward of Lord Maskullance. She was what an aristocrat should be, porcelain and silk, unreachable, gracious, untainted by the dust of all this common death.

On an early autumn evening, when a few swallows were performing the last dance in the sky, the penultimate act of the Maskullance saga was visited on Bleston. He did not anticipate any such thing. He had been out shooting in neighbouring parts and come back in a rage because his viciousness was unmatched by any knack with a gun.

Dinner had been served at an earlier hour of late, for Lord Maskullance had claimed an increasing tiredness.

They met then in the dining room, these remaining three, his lordship, Bleston, and beauteous Louisa in a low-cut gown of dark mourning, a broach and necklace of jade and jet.

They dined in silence, but for the twelve or twenty morose tirades of Bleston concerning useless keepers, feckless beaters, and imaginary prey.

The concluding savoury was served. The servants left the room.

"What's this muck? Alice is getting as useless as Crapp."

Lord Maskullance addressed Louisa across the table's length.

"The sadness of the summer's passing. The apples in the orchard are red, and they fall. Are we all merely apples, Louisa? Ripened for death and devouring?"

"Even the rose must die," said Louisa, between the books and the experimental dialogue Lord Maskullance had always encouraged in her.

"But the rose won't die. My white rose with the black hair. I can predict for her a long and lustrous life."

Bleston snorted.

"I'll take some brandy, uncle."

"Of course you will, Bleston. Tell me, Louisa, how do you think such a fine young man as our Bleston deserves to meet his end?"

Bleston looked round, infuriated.

"Is that your humour, sir?"

"Yes, Bleston, it is. Just as your humour was to go gaming after the funeral of your mother and aunt."

"Which you didn't attend, uncle."

"I am old and feeble. I shall soon join the ladies in the dark. I don't hurry to funerals, one hurries towards *me*."

"Hungch," agreed Bleston.

"Well, then, Louisa," said Lord Maskullance, "what so you think? A soft and gentle death for my nephew, or a theatrical and epic death?"

Louisa considered, her lashes lowered, candlelight swimming in the lagoons of eyes.

"Nothing soft," she murmured at last, "for such a bold gentleman."

"Well said," barked Bleston, missing the point.

He pulled the brandy decanter back to him and refilled his glass attentively.

"Well, Louisa," said Lord Maskullance. "One should not be dilatory."

Louisa raised her eyes. Between peridot and amber they shone upon the old man with as much love as she was capable of—indeed, not much, and yet, by its very dearth, valuable.

"Dilatory," said Bleston, shifting his fat body. "I recall meeting this minx on the moor, a mermaiden in the rain." He belched loudly, without bothering to pretend.

"Louisa will fill your glass again, Bleston," said Lord Maskullance. "Get up and come to the window with me. We'll observe the park, how the dusk settles on it. Louisa must work her magic unseen."

Bleston said, "Why should I move?"

"Because I tell you to, because you are a gentleman and have impeccable manners."

"Hah," said Bleston, but he laughed and rose and went to the windows and stood there with the old man by him. And Louisa, who carried her phial now always with her, prepared the glass of brandy in her own unique way.

She had not tried again to poison Sheepshead. He had ceased following her. Seldom was Lord Maskullance able to walk with her about the gardens, but when he did, the figure of the butler-steward, his snuff and humbugs, were not to be seen. Sheepshead might wait. It was right that he should, until the opus of Maskullance be concluded.

Lord Maskullance guided Bleston back to the table. "And there is your drink, Bleston." Prepared by magic.

Bleston took the brandy and drained it and poured himself another.

"We must gather the apples," said Lord Maskullance to Louisa. "Do you think an apple has a soul?"

"Does a man have one?" asked Louisa. She was not expressly watchful. She saw that the old man was not either. Each knew or had deduced the oncoming fury.

"One hopes not," said his lordship. "One hopes for rest. The soul, if it exists, must surely undergo such—"

Bleston gave a loud cough. He put his hand to his throat and half got up. "This brandy," he said and choked.

"—such endless toils and tasks to purify and make sense of itself. I confess," confessed Lord Maskullance as Bleston arched across the table, cartwheeled among the candles and descended to the floor, taking plates and cutlery and table-cloth with him, "I confess I long for oblivion."

"Oh no," said Louisa. "Whatever the punishment, I long to live for ever, however I may, and in whatever form."

Bleston kicked and streams of crockery and blood hit the ceiling.

"The form in your case would be exquisite, Louisa. I think perhaps your soul would resemble a small furry animal, an ermine or white fox."

Bleston rolled into the fire-place and the fire screen fell with a crash. None of the blood had touched Lord Maskullance or Louisa. A last candle tottered and fell to extinguishment.

"I shouldn't mind," said Louisa, "so long as I was able to remember myself."

"And a mirror. You must have that. A mirror in Hell, which will be your home."

"Oh, Hell, do you think?" Louisa flirted with dismay.

They gazed at one another, and Bleston's right boot shot off and kicked over a vase of chrysanthemums on the sideboard.

There was silence.

"Obviously an apoplexy. No need to call out the doctor so late," said Lord Maskullance. "It will wait till morning." Lord Maskullance rose. He said, "Louisa, when I saw you on the moor, when I beheld your beauty, I knew that you were death. And so I invited you in. In half an hour, will you come to my bed chamber? You know you need fear nothing from me, from an old man, who, besides, has never seen women in that fashion."

"I shall," she said, "of course."

"My lovely one," he said. "Be swift."

But when Louisa went along the corridor to the vast old

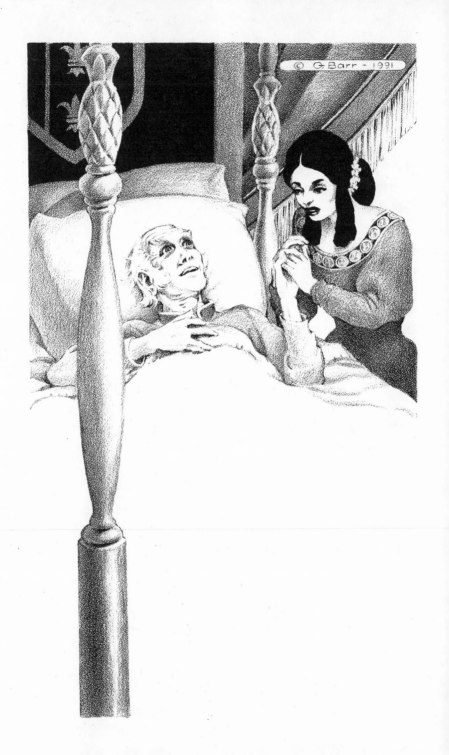

bedroom with its vast old bed draped round in velvets, she found the ancient man lying on his pillows laughing, quietly and riotously, shaking from head to foot with joy.

"Oh Louisa, my Louisa, my darling death. What delight I've had from you."

She went to him and of her own accord she took his skeleton hand, like a dry white autumn leaf. She held his hand as it and he shuddered with laughter, and then he lay back and only smiled and closed his eyes. Presently his features sunk inwards, like spoiled dough. So easily he went, and without her assistance. Lord Maskullance had laughed himself to sleep for ever.

Louisa was questioned concerning the murder of Lord Maskullance on a rainy misty morning when the oaks and beeches bled with leaves. She had been seen going to his room. She was suspected of smothering him with a pillow.

An inquest had been held. Despite slight postmortem evidence, it was concluded that Lord Maskullance might well have died of suffocation. Though there were few if any definite indications, the circumstances were extremely suspicious. The body of Bleston also seemed worthy of thorough examination, and it provided a more sinister picture. The spine was snapped, the wind-pipe collapsed, and there were haemorrhages from both lungs and abdomen. On the orders of the coroner the other bodies of the luckless family were next exhumed and a more detailed autopsy performed on each of them. These yielded results only sensibly consequent to their modes of death. However, Georgie's injuries were now viewed in an altered light. He had been thrown from a horse, which could well have occasioned his broken back, and the haemorrhaging of stomach, lungs and trachea. Yet these lesions were so like those

Bleston had incurred, who had not been thrown from a horse at all, but was supposed to have suffered an apoplectic fit, as to give rise to query on both counts. Agathena's injuries were consistent with having fallen down stairs. And yet it might be said that she had been most unfortunate, for persons had actually fallen down the same stair before, with only sprained or broken limbs as a result. Maud and Millicent were mysterious in that such little or no amounts of liquid were found in the lungs. 'Dry' drowning no longer seemed a full explanation. Had all three ladies been dead before their falls into air, water and soup?

For traces of poison the pathologists therefore searched diligently. They found none.

In the case of Bleston strychnine was suspected, but no hint could be obtained, even though the corpse was fresh. Nor was the body of Lord Maskullance any use either on that score. Were perhaps suffocation, and poisons of two different types employed?

Further investigations went on. It was the most prolonged inquest the county had seen. A tobacconist, who had perished during the season of the other deaths, the lunatic found on the moor with edibles from the manor, the peculiarly-dead policeman, they were also exhumed. As were the bodies of an elderly lady formerly living in the vicinity of the manor, a thatcher from the village who had died during the building of a cottage by tumbling off the roof, and a blacksmith, thought drunk, who had fallen down a chimney.

The situation was so strange by now, nevertheless, and the countryside in such uproar about the case, that Louisa, who had given evidence only of amazed innocence and genteel bewilderment, was committed for trial on the coroner's warrant.

The streets of the town were not paved with gold.

*   *   *

60

am not guilty."

Louisa stood upright, a white flower face upon a mid-night mourning stem, in the prisoner's dock. Her dignity and loveliness inspired cartoonists all about the court, and in the public gallery gave rise both to jealous dislike and adoring chivalry.

This one statement, invited from her by the judge, was all she was to say. Her own statement of innocence followed the statement of the crimes of which she stood accused. That she had murdered Lord Maskullance by applying a pillow to his sleeping face and in some other form or forms dispatched all the residents of Maskullance who had shared with her in the bulk of the will of the late Lord. Sole inheritrix she would not be, save for some small bequests to servants, and the equal portion of Mr. Sheeps-head the butler-steward of the estate. This was motive enough.

The Crown opened the prosecution of Louisa with every witness reckoned at its disposal. On the stand before her Louisa beheld the maids of the house, Alice and the scullery maids, the footmen, Mrs. Crampp (much worn down and mostly incoherent), village acquaintances of the dead tobacconist, the old lady, the thatcher, and the blacksmith, none of which latter knew anything of Louisa, although they were sometimes led to think they did: Her own counsel swiftly intervening.

Louisa's barrister was a Mr. Meadham Trevis. He had taken the case on seeing Louisa's picture in a newspaper. He was himself a flamboyant and handsome man, rising rapidly in his profession. He had seldom lost a case and declared Louisa's to be a challenge. "Everything is against her," he had said, "except her beauty and the law of coincidence. That's what I shall seek to prove. That lightning does strike twice and indeed in this instance at least six times."

He himself had been struck by Louisa's poise. At no moment

did she seem in despair or even uncertainty. Although she did not tell him so, it was as if she believed God Himself would protect her in her blamelessness. She was also inscrutable, a quality Mr. Trevis, who collected jade figures, liked.

All that the manor servants could say of Louisa was that she had entered into the house in a curious and rather outlandish way, and that she had never revealed her origins. The prosecution of course made much of this. But Mr. Trevis, in cross-examination, was able always to bring out that Louisa was obviously also a lady of great breeding, who had appeared devoted to Lord Maskullance, in whom possibly she had alone confided. And while the others had shown her off-hand or variable behaviour, she had stayed courteous and serene at all times. Was this the mark of a malcontent?

There was additionally, as Mr. Trevis stressed via the witnesses, firm evidence to support the natural theory of all the extraordinary plethora of deaths. (He excluded from the itinerary the tobacconist, lunatic, policeman, thatcher, old lady and blacksmith with sublime contempt. Was Louisa to be responsible for everything, even perhaps to the dead sheep found on the moor, or a local chicken dispatched for a roast? The gallery laughed.) The groom called to testify to Georgie's horsemanship was made to admit that Georgie ill-treated his mounts, and that the grey would sweat and roll its eyes in fear if he even passed the stable door. Lord Maskullance had refused to have the animal destroyed after Georgie's fall. Georgie, had said his lordship, had driven the poor brute to do it. Maud meanwhile had exhibited an erratic mood before her drowning, as the maid who had waited at dinner could confirm. Maud had seemed suicidally inclined, even refusing a meal, a thing unheard of. The shock of the lake water stopping her heart, killing the victim before any fluid could be ingested into the lungs, was not unknown. Agathena meanwhile could well have missed her footing on the stairs in her quite-to-be expected state of extreme grief on which everyone agreed. Millicent had fainted at this horror, as Alice had soon after, and the tureen unfortunately took its toll. Had Millicent's face not been partially scalded? This trauma alone might account for her demise. Which left only Bleston. He was, according to the doctor summoned to describe his wounds, a perfect candidate for apoplexy. In a violent fit he might easily have damaged himself fatally in falling over the table into the fireplace— as Louisa in her written statement had explained and of which evidence had abounded. Otherwise Lord Maskullance was an old man. So many awful shocks could well have seen off a younger stronger one.

The case so far had run two days, the jury each night being imprisoned in a local hotel, Louisa being returned to the adjacent jail. Here her wardresses, taking her for a perfect lady, treated her with careful consideration.

"My plan," said Mr. Trevis to Louisa in the grey confines of her cell, "is that I shall call no defence witness, and neither will I call on you to make any further statement. That way, I'll have the final word at the summing up."

He had noticed the judge was already partial to Louisa, saying she was pale and might sit down, and once intervening in the cross-examination to stress a point Mr. Trevis was already making to Louisa's good. The jury, like the gallery, was a blend of entranced and disapproving. This might prove a nuisance.

"My one worry," lied Mr. Trevis, "is that the prosecution have up their sleeve an ultimate witness who must in some way have information that might discredit you or show you in a bad light. This Sheepshead, the butler. Would you say that he was in your favour?"

"I think, sir, he was envious of my closeness to Lord Maskullance."

"I was afraid of that. Well, I must simply sharpen my pruning knife."

Louisa smiled a little. She had received that morning a letter from Mr. Sheepshead. It informed her that he would call on her, by way of some special dispensation of the prison, that evening.

And from this, if from no other thing, Louisa knew herself as ever still in the supporting hand of fate.

Mr. Trevis rose to leave her, tickled as always by this succulent and placid calm in the face of such odds. His gaze swept over the tiny shelf on which, partly against the rules, a few feminine articles had been allowed, even a small perfume bottle of clear glass, perhaps thought too tiny to cause harm.

After he had left her, Louisa picked up the poison phial and sniffed it. It smelled of the perfume with which she had rubbed its outer surface on the morning of her arrest.

In the grey cell, as daintily as in her Blue Room, she awaited the fateful visitor.

He came at eight. He sat down at the long table facing Louisa, and the wardress whom Louisa had charmed the most stood well back at the door. She was a little deaf.

"You should speak loudly," said Louisa, "so the wardress can hear you, Sheepshead."

"No need for that, said Sheepshead. "My words are for you alone." His spectacles gleamed, and she knew herself, as one infallibly does at last, in the presence of the inimical enemy. "Miss Louisa," said Sheepshead, "you are a murderess. I know it. I've seen you. Not the means, never that. But your goings to and fro. You were with Mr. Georgie when he rode along the beech walk. You were with Miss Maud beside the lake. You were with the ladies, both of them, before their fatal falls, above in the room of one, and below with the other as we ran, the rest of us, into the hall. And Mr. Bleston, you were in the dining room with him, also. His lordship was there. He too perhaps saw what you did.

And so his lordship you murdered, for I was the one that saw you pass into his bed chamber by candlelight, where no lady should go by herself."

Louisa lowered her eyes, modestly.

Sheepshead put between them on the table a large bag of humbugs.

The wardress was alerted and said, "Nothing must change hands.

"I assure you, madam, that it won't," said Sheepshead. He looked at Louisa from his blind glass lens eyes. "You'd like to doctor them, no doubt. The poor fellow in the shop succumbed to your scheme for me, did he not? And the madman with my slice of the cake, and the poor man with the whistle meant for my mouth. What did you use, I wonder?"

"I think," said Louisa primly, "you accuse me of witchcraft."

"Fifty years ago, maybe. Now I make other plans. What are they? I've only to speak. At best they'll think you have the power to drive men and women to their ends. It will condemn you. Even if I never see you hanged, Miss Louisa, my evidence will be enough to keep you incarcerated for the length of your wicked life."

"It was kind of you to warn me."

"Don't mention it, miss."

And from his coat Sheepshead drew the habitual box of his snuff, and taking in his triumph an extra large double pinch, he sniffed it up.

And then, Sheepshead sneezed.

It was not general with him, snuff-accustomed as he was, to sneeze. It took him by surprise. Perhaps in his nervous malice he had overcharged the dose. His glasses slipped, his head shook violently sideways, eyes closed and mouth wide open.

Louisa's hand in turn darted forward. She too was excessive in excitement. One, two, *three* lights flashed in the air.

65

Sheepshead opened his watery small nearly sightless eyes to find she extended to him her lace handkerchief.

"God bless you, Sheepshead."

"Was it a sneeze?" asked the deaf wardress. "God bless you, sir."

Sheepshead stared at the handkerchief. Then he smiled, pushed up his glasses, and waved the lace away. "I thank you. *No.*" He thrust back his chair. "Nothing must change hands. But you can keep the humbugs."

Louisa inclined her head, a noble rival in honorable defeat.

"You mustn't blame me, Sheepshead, for my try."

"There, there," said the wardress, mistaking Sheepshead's blowing nose as he left the cell, "don't take it too hard. Do you know why we say *bless you* at a sneeze? It's because the Devil tries to enter in at one!"

"Just so," said Sheepshead.

"And blessing makes him fail."

"*Just* so."

keletal sunlight, thin, bright and hard, laid its mesh upon the courtroom as Louisa the dark and fair came into the dock. Escorted by her wardresses, she was like a tragic queen flanked by raven attendants. Her face had stayed flawless in innocence, and if she was not redolent of absolute homely goodness, yet she seemed pure, beyond the world, saint-like; holy.

Handsome Meadham Trevis, her knight, offered her the smallest and most gentlemanly sign of courtesy and kindness.

The judge burned his hearty Christmas red.

The prosecution called at once for Mr. Sheepshead. Mr. Sheepshead, fortified by snuff and humbugs in the anteroom, entered.

"Mr. Sheepshead, you were I believe Lord Maskullance's

butler, and later also his steward, for some fifteen years. Is that so?"

"Yes. And before that a servant at the house."

"Which would seem to place you in an excellent position to know the ways of his lordship and the household in general."

Mr. Sheepshead affirmed that he felt it did.

"How then did you react, when the young woman, identified only as 'Louisa', was brought into the house?"

"I was at a loss, sir. But then, I trusted my master. He seemed to value the young lady, and I could do no less than show her every respect."

"The lady to whom you refer is here in the court?"

Sheepshead indicated Louisa.

And Louisa looked upon him in turn and observable on her crystalline face was the faintest disappointment, but only for an instant.

"Louisa then was the companion, and subsequently became the ward, of your master, Lord Maskullance. She was put into his will."

Sheepshead agreed.

"Did this enrage you?"

"Not at all, sir. It made no difference to my portion."

"Did it, though, occur to you, Mr. Sheepshead, when Mr. George, and later Miss Maud, met their violent deaths, that by the arrangement of the will more was then to be shared by the remaining parties?"

"It did not, directly, occur to me. However, had I considered it, I should have known that it was so."

"And do you imagine, Mr. Sheepshead, that this thought also occurred to Miss Louisa?"

"I object, my lord," said Meadham Trevis, rising like a gaunt and elegant heron from his seat. "My honourable friend requires his witness to be a telepath."

67

"Quite so," admonished the judge. "The prosecution will be wary."

The prosecution bowed. The point had been made, discounted or not.

Sheepshead was then questioned on the demeanour of Louisa during the series of savage and distressing deaths.

"I can't say, sir, very much on the lady's demeanour. She was at all times very calm, as now, when she's at trial for her life."

"You've said in your written statement, Mr. Sheepshead, that Louisa was always, and I must repeat, *always*, in the vicinity of those who perished exactly prior to their deaths."

A murmurous rumble went through the court and was rapped to silence.

Sheepshead nodded. "On every occasion."

"You must describe these occasions."

Mr. Sheepshead did so. He reported spying Louisa on the beech walk with Mr. Georgie minutes before the horse apparently threw him. He described Louisa with Miss Maud upon the terrace, closeted in the Blue Room, and later travelling through the park late at night, towards the lake.

"How did it happen, Mr. Sheepshead, that you were also near at hand that evening?"

"I took an interest in the coverts and had gone to inspect them after dark as a fox had been seen."

Mr. Sheepshead went on to say that Louisa had also gone up to Agathena's room and stayed some while, about an hour and a half before Agathena's plummet down the stairs. No one else had gone near Agathena at that time. Louisa was also the last to leave the room where Millicent had fainted and might have manhandled her into the tureen. Louisa had also taken some of Millicent's medicine and might have tampered with it.

"We have no evidence of poison, Mr. Sheepshead."

Sheepshead spoke boldly. "She told me herself, sir, that I would take her for a witch."

A sort of gasp now from the gallery. Witchcraft, like headless horses and webbed-foot men of the mire was obsolete, yet scarcely forgotten.

Meadham Trevis said, "Mr. Sheepshead will have a witness, I trust, to this latest accusation."

Mr. Sheepshead had not, however, or at least none that was useable.

In the matter of Bleston, Louisa had been in the exact room during the young man's 'fit'. Lord Maskullance was also there and, once Louisa had visited him improperly in his bed chamber, Lord Maskullance too lay dead.

When Sheepshead had finished, a pall of expectant horror crouched over the court. The judge frowned. The jury quivered. Only Louisa appeared unmoved, although she watched Sheepshead almost without blinking. Delay might have been anticipated, but this was great delay. And had the damage been done?

"Lastly, Mr. Sheepshead, did you throughout this time go in fear for your own life?"

"I believe that she practiced against me, but I was saved by accident. The tobacconist died in my place, I think. The lunatic had been given food intended for me. And my whistle."

Mr. Trevis rose to cross-examine.

"Mr. Sheepshead, under the terms of the will, I understand that whoever was left alive, should other parties not endure, would receive the bulk of the estate and monies. Am I correct?"

"Yes, sir, you are."

"And you also are a beneficiary, are you not?"

"I am. His lordship was so good."

"Then, not to put a fine point on it, you, as much as this hapless girl, are set to inherit a far larger amount than you would have done had all these other unhappy persons survived."

From the gallery there was a cheer. It was brusquely shushed.

"It's true that I stand to inherit a larger portion now."

"Well, we will leave that a moment. I wish to inquire, Mr. Sheepshead, if you believed this young girl strove to murder you, why you took no steps to protect yourself—I do not mention your employers—by seeking the help of the police?"

Mr. Sheepshead paused in thought. It was genuine. He said, "These things were a family matter."

"Oh, come, Mr. Sheepshead. I am to credit that, with a rampant witch-murderess upon your track, and your master's life in danger, you *hesitated*?"

"I did, sir. I regret, I had no proof."

"Indeed," said Mr. Trevis. "You had *not*. And let that too, pray, be noted." And he grinned at the gallery at least two thirds of which was now applauding him.

The judge suggested clearing the court of hooligans and pin-drop quiet fell.

"Mr. Sheepshead," said Mr. Trevis, "I brought myself to this court to defend the stainless character of a young girl. A girl perhaps mysterious because she has chosen to keep close past sorrows and to protect others than herself from prying eyes. A girl who has been pilloried by persons in this court for her honour in silence. I have no intention of breaching Louisa's privacy. I have no intention even of calling upon her to make a statement. Her face speaks for itself. Whoever looks at her and does not see true purity, pure honesty, an unsmirched soul, is a beast and a madman, and I believe that none so base, foul or misdirected sits here in judgement today. With such a jury I need only say, *Look at her!* She needs no other defence. She need say no other word. Her being is evidence enough. But for you, sir," and here Mr. Trevis drew himself up towering to his full, black winged height, "*you*. I would suggest that, steeped in jealousy and avarice, you have used this faultless girl, who has suffered enough in seeing

70

a whole family made dear to her and then swept away, as a decoy for your own villainy. I suggest that if any fashioned a crime, it was you yourself. God knows how you did them, these heartless evil acts. But in your place you have planted Louisa. We have your word that she was here, and here, and here. But if she was there, then so were you. And could it not have *been* you? Have you not, strong old man that you are, twice the strength of delicate Louisa, to fling a man from a horse, to thrust a maiden in a lake, to doctor medicine and alcohol in such a way—perfidious and incredible—that death followed. And have not you, sir, the power of manner to send a woman crazed by the grief of losing two of her children to fling herself to her doom down the stairs? Or to press a traitor's pillow to a sleeping, trusting face? And sir, pray tell me, if Louisa is sent to the gallows, who is it that will then inherit *all* of Maskullance?"

Mr. Sheepshead stood dumbfounded. He took out his handkerchief and mopped his brow. Visibly he flushed and sweated.

"You have called this immaculate girl a witch. What then may *you* be?" Mr. Trevis raised his marvelous and thunderous voice, "May you not be a *devil*? A devil, sir, who cannot even endure the name of God?" And Mr. Trevis pointed his long finger at Sheepshead. "Answer then, in *God's name*, Mr. Sheepshead!"

Sheepshead's eyes bulged. He seemed to swell. He jerked at his cravat. He looked like nothing so much as a bullfrog. His lips opened.

Two or three women screamed.

For out of Sheepshead's mouth there dazzled a blue flame, like the forked tongue of lightning.

Three or four seconds he stood there, the blue lights running out of him, his lips and nostrils and ears, and around the eggs of his poached eyes. And then, and then Mr. Sheepshead—exploded. He burst into a gush of flame that enveloped him from the belly to the crown of his head. His arms were waving flags of flame. His legs buckled and he collapsed, and gouts of incendiary matter burst off him and were fired to all four corners of the court.

Nearly all the women were shrieking, the men howling. There was a panic rush towards the doors. The police struggled. Young lawyers hid beneath benches. The judge rose like a red carnival, goggling. The press screeched. Only Louisa and Mr. Meadham Trevis preserved their dignity. One in great shock, believing he had caused this. The other knowing quite well that she had.

Three drops, had said her aunt, *and there's fire.*

The newspapers were to adopt the story with fiendish glee, gloating on every detail as the tissues of Mr. Sheepshead burned and were consumed. Spontaneous combustion was known of, but had seldom if ever occurred before so many spectators.

She had dropped them in his snuff. She had gambled, (she was canny at games) that inhalation at the nose, as ingestion at the eyes, would suffice. She had not known how long it would require. He might have taken a pinch last night and died. As it happened he had gone up at the ideal moment. An act of God. Trial by ordeal.

Meadham Trevis was made.

Louisa would, the next day, be set free.

When she returned to Maskullance, a downpour deluged the landscape of the moor.

It seemed to Louisa, as she passed the red stones at the wayside, that now and then she saw on them a cloaked figure, sitting patiently. But she had no intention of stopping the carriage.

*   *   *

he manor lay under the midnight rain. Out of the black vegetable of it only two or three windows bloomed with loving lamplight. All the servants, but for the footman Podgers, Prudent and Alice, were dismissed. New servants could be hired very easily, and for now Louisa had chosen of those who had tried to be loyal to her. The rest, sent away with their meagre expectations of the will, had streamed into splashing darkness and were gone.

Above the main door, the golden ram's mask wept water. The other masks, skulls and lances dripped and spouted. The mullioned windows showed their spectacle lenses of blank eyes to the night.

Louisa was in the parlour. She had eaten her dinner there, a delightful dinner cooked gratefully by Alice. Louisa wore blackest mourning of moiré silk, a necklace and ear-drops of diamonds. Her hair was loose, and she sat combing it now before the fire.

Louisa was happy. Her happiness is hard to describe, or comprehend. The wolf who has killed the lamb and feasts on its chops can feel no pain. And somewhere through the shadows of the house she dreaded no ghostly step. To hear dim echoes of Lord Maskullance, laughing, would only have pleased her.

Midnight then. A little red wine in the goblet, a late peach from the hothouse on a plate. The firelight licking with its amber at the chimney.

And from the front of the house a great loud knocking.

Did Louisa start? No. But she turned her silken head, and her hair, more moiré than the moiré, shawled over her.

Podgers came to the parlour door. "Someone's out there in the rain, Miss Louisa."

"Then go and see to it."

And Podgers, who *was* afraid for reasons he could not explain and that had nothing to do with the hour's lateness or the six murders and one explosion, or the lunatic asylum even, went to the door where the bell had not been jangled and opened it.

And Podgers jumped back in alarm. And again, did not know why.

But there at the door stood a man. A large man with a head, a mane, of tawny hair, dressed in a suit of black velvet, a snow of lace, a waist-coat striped like a tiger, and on his hand a ring of tigerseye that winked and fleered and *shone.*

"A fine night," said this man, and Podgers cowered. Knowing now. For there was no carriage anywhere, and the man who had come stepping through the rain in his buckled shoes, he had not a drop of moisture on him. "I'm here to see the mistress of the house."

"Miss—Louisa."

"Louisa. Yes."

And so final was that 'yes' that Podgers stood back, and in walked the big black and tawny dry tiger of a man, and going by, went unerringly towards the parlour, waving Podgers away, so Podgers *ran.*

Louisa looked up as the door opened again.

"Madam," said the figure and bowed to her, smiling. He was large and he was beautiful, with eyes like a fine old brandy. "May I come in?"

"I think I can't keep you out," said Louisa. Who though she had never worshipped planets, was yet a daughter of the supernatural mire. She did not need to believe in the Devil to acknowledge his minions, if she met them.

The demon, if such he was, came and sat opposite her, cozily across the hearth. And here he tried the wine and ate one half of the peach, cutting it neatly with a silver knife, straight through the stone.

"Now Louisa," he said, "why am I here?" Louisa lowered her eyes and fanned herself with a wisp of lace. "*Now*, Louisa.

Louisa looked up. "To take me down to Hell?" she asked.

The demon—perhaps he was—gave a great and vehement laugh, which was heard all the way to the belowstairs, where Alice fainted again, and some cakes were burnt.

"Yes, yes, Louisa, you will go to Hell. But have no fear. Hell, you'll find, is an excellent place. Believe me, the streets are truly paved with gold, which though in places is molten, picturesque detours are provided. Heaven I think you would find a touch insipid. The climate isn't all it is said to be. Chilly, Louisa. And the air rather on the thin side. But there are exotic plants in Hell and the most enchanting volcanoes."

"Surely," said Louisa, "Hell is a spot for punishment."

"Only of those who fall into the clutches of Hell's demons and haven't pleased. You, dear Louisa, will be an honoured guest."

"I've only your word for it."

"This is so. But then. Think of the help you have so far had. Isn't this a token of fair treatment to come?"

"Perhaps," said Louisa.

"Besides, you must consider this, that perhaps these people, and others also, have owed you their lives."

"How can that be?"

"Dear Louisa, if you must ask, I have no means to explain."

The demon, (he should be reckoned one) gazed at Louisa, and the firelight showed burning towers in his eyes.

"Why then," said Louisa, " you here, sir? So very late."

"To congratulate you, Louisa," said the demon. "And to wish you well in your future career, as a serpent among men."

"Thank you," said Louisa.

"It is my pleasure," said the demon.

"And is that all?"

"Dear Louisa," said the demon, "how exquisitely straightforward. Yes. It's all. Quite all."

And so saying he stepped into the fire and in a rush of tiger sparks was gone.

Louisa ate the other half of the peach, (though not the stone as the demon had) and drank the last of her wine.

Taking a candle, she went her way up the stairs of Maskullance, to her Blue Room of bluebirds and cornflowers, She sang a little as she went, and through the noise of the winter dawn of rain and wind, her voice was sweet as the music of the stars.

The End